Lessons From A Dinosaur: Listening

Printed in the United States of America
First printing, 2013

ISBN-13: 978-1533068743

ISBN-10: 1533068747

Name the types of dinosaurs!

Triceratops

Ankylosaurus

Brontosaurus

The (Tyrannosaurus) Rex family
Diddy Rex, Lil Rex & Big Momma Rex

Big Momma Rex walked into the room, "Good Morning, Lil Rex!"

Grrr... Lil Rex wasn't listening, he just wanted to sleep.

"Lil Rex?" Big Momma Rex repeated herself.

Lil Rex wasn't listening, he was busy playing with his toys.

Big Momma Rex just wanted Lil Rex to listen.

"What do you want to do today?" asked Big Momma Rex.
Lil Rex thought about it. "I want to go to the playground!"

"Sorry Lil Rex, the playground is closed today because it's being fixed, maybe you can go next week. How about playing here at home with your friends?"

But Lil Rex wasn't listening, he was too busy thinking about going down the slide and building castles in the sandbox.

Lil Rex ran past his mom and out of the house. He wasn't listening at all!

What would happen to him?

"Whoa there, Lil Rex!" Anky the Ankylosaurus was fixing up the playground. "This place is closed! We're fixing it up!"

But Lil Rex still wasn't listening. All he wanted to do was play!

Lil Rex first ran past Anky, then up onto the playground...

...and crashed to the ground!

"OUCH! My arm!" Lil Rex yelled for help. "Somebody help me please!"

Big Momma Rex rushed to the playground.
"Where is my baby? I heard him crying!"

"He just fell off the playground!" Anky replied.

"Mommy, I'm covered in sand and my arm hurts real bad."

"Here, let me help you, Lil Rex." Momma Rex helped him up and decided to bring him to the doctor to make sure he was alright.

"Well, your arm is sprained but it will heal with time. This large bandage will keep it protected. Next time listen to your mom." The doctor was very serious.

Lil Rex was sad. He knew he should have listened.

When they got home the Rex family had a little talk. "Lil Rex, your mother and I are very concerned. This wouldn't have happened if you would have listened."

We want you to have fun Lil Rex, but we also want you to be safe because we love you so much. That's why it's so important for you to pay attention when we talk to you.

"I'm really sorry I didn't listen. I know I should have. From now on I promise I will because you only want what's best for me. Can I go play now?"

"Of course, now that you've learned your lesson you can go play." Big Mamma and Diddy Rex both agreed.

Lil Rex went back to play but his arm started hurting and he was in pain.

Big Momma Rex came into the room. "Lil Rex, I have some medicine for you that will help your arm feel better."

Lil Rex didn't want to take the medicine
because he thought it tasted bad.

But he remembered that his parents only loved him and cared for him.
So he listened and took the medicine.

Even though it didn't taste very good he was very happy he listened because his arm started feeling better!

"See? Listening is good, isn't it?" Big Momma Rex wanted to make sure Lil Rex understood.

He happily agreed, listening is good.

"You're tired and it's been a long day.
Let's get you tucked into bed."

Lil Rex listened.

"What did you learn today Lil Rex?"

"I learned to always _____ to mommy and daddy." Lil Rex responded, "And always send someone else to the playground BEFORE I go!"

They both laughed together. "You're truly wonderful and so special to me, I love you so much, Lil Rex."
"I love you too, Mommy!"

"Goodnight and sleep well, son."
And that's exactly what he did.

THE END

THANK YOU for purchasing and reading Lessons From A Dinosaur: Listening! A lot of hard work went into creating it, so if you enjoyed it, please consider writing a review. Your review makes a HUGE difference and will help others enjoy it in the future.

Authors like me depend on you and your reviews – even if it's only a sentence – so please take a minute to let everyone know that you enjoyed this book.

I love creating new ebooks and I'm always curious about what readers want to see next from me. If you have any ideas, questions or concerns, or just want to stay in the loop, you can reach me at: shannonkempenich@gmail.com
I read every email I get.
Thanks again and I hope to hear from you!

P.S. Don't forget to check out our other books!

Made in the USA
Columbia, SC
15 October 2020